For my greatest fan always, anywhere...
For my big sister, Diane.
—*David*

To my parents, whose love has
always added colour to my visions.
—*Michael*

Beach City (detail)

Moonlighter

Hi Geraldine

Many thanks for the loan. Having now been there, I can see how the writing & paintings match. Very good!

For us it was very hot while we were there & very dry - Fire risk! Highly unusual.

Thanks. John

The Colours of

BRITISH COLUMBIA

Sunstruck

The Colours of
BRITISH COLUMBIA

by David Bouchard

with paintings by Michael Tickner

RAINCOAST BOOKS

Vancouver

To Geraldine, may you enjoy all the colours of life! Michael Tickner

FIRST PUBLISHED IN CANADA IN 1994 BY

Raincoast Book Distribution Ltd.
8680 Cambie Street
Vancouver, BC V6P 6M9

Designed by Dean Allen
Set in Monotype Bembo

CANADIAN CATALOGUING IN PUBLICATION DATA

Bouchard, Dave, 1952-
The colours of British Columbia

ISBN 1-895714-52-4

1. British Columbia — Poetry. 2. British Columbia in art.
I. Tickner, Michael, 1947- II. Title.
PS8553.O759C64 1994   C811'.54   C94-910270-9
PR9199.3.B68C64 1994

Printed and bound in Hong Kong through Mandarin Offset.

1 3 5 7 9 10 8 6 4 2

This book is printed on paper produced from selectively harvested trees. No clearcut, rainforest or other
endangered species products were used. The manufacturing process involves no dioxin-producing chlorine.

Michael Tickner's fine art is available in original paintings, limited
edition silkscreens and lithograph reproductions.

For further enquiries please contact:

I Art Publishing Limited Prints
Box 396, Lions Bay, BC VON 2EO
(604) 921-7865

When you come to our province, you come knowing colour,
    the way you have seen it at home.

Rich – and clear – and a part of the memory you'll cherish some day
    on your own.

But don't just take pictures – to do B.C. justice you'll need more
    than tracings of light.

There's more to our colour than pictures can show, you'll need to use
    more than mere sight.

I remember when I first saw mountains and lakes, our forests, our
    ocean and shores.

I was used to the colours I'd brought from the prairie and thought
    that I'd see little more.

But soon shortly after, I saw a new colour and wondered what more
    there could be.

Let me now tell you, while fresh in my memory, I found my first
    colour in trees.

Two Close In

You might have seen green in hedges or valleys, in grasses, in
   parks or the plain.

But you don't have the slightest idea of what green is unless you
   have stood in the rain:

Stood deep in the forest and looked up at tall trees, so green you
   can feel they're alive.

Emily Carr shows the green as we see it – a colour trying hard
   to survive.

*I remember the first time I walked through the forest and lifted my
   head to the sky.*

*I remember the soft rays of sun as they crept through the branches
   that gathered up high.*

*I remember my words and my thoughts this first day – "Carr has
   painted the truth!"*

*A vibrance so green that it has to be seen … it was much like the
   green of my youth.*

Green Forever

When you try to look back at your memories of red, or the
  visions you have of your home,

You'll probably remember clowns at the circus or toys that
  were lost as you've grown.

But for those of us here whom you ask, "What's your red?"
  after thought we will all say the same.

It's always the colour we see in the evening, a sunset so often
  aflame.

*It's the kind of red sunset you might find on postcards, the kind that
  will have people say:*

*"It's just like a picture, painted on velvet, but it really can't look quite
  this way…"*

Well, it does *look like velvet, it* does *look like dreams, and it* does
  have that mystical look,

*Of dragons and castles and princes and fairies and places seen only
  in books.*

Late Set

You can always find tulips by thousands in Holland each spring
    as so many folks do.

But come to the West Coast not long after Christmas and you'll come to know
    yellow here too.

We know we're the envy of all of our neighbours who can't help but wish
    they were here.

When their winter hangs on and our flowers abound is the time when
    our yellow is dear.

*I remember the first time I saw yellow tulips on sidewalks in quaint
    Dundarave,*

*Like thousands of others who'd come from the East to escape from
    the cold winter's rage.*

*I remember my words and my thoughts that spring day: "This truly is
    heaven on earth."*

*Yellow's the colour of spring every year, it's the colour that brings
    us new birth.*

A Rush of Spring

And what about blue? You might think, "The sky!"– that's a blue that is
    known everywhere.

Or the ocean, of course, on a bright sunny day, is a blue world
    of water and air.

But for those of us here who wake every day in the fresh crisp
    air of this land,

It's the blue that we find on the tarps in the bay, when you see
    that blue you'll understand.

I remember the first time I rounded the bend and came right up to
    the pier.

I remember the chill of that morning in winter, the damp and the
    frost were so clear.

I remember my words and my thoughts that cold day, "I've never seen
    such clear blue."

It was as deep and as rich as the lakes in our northlands, and I can now
    share it with you.

Winter Blues

Somewhat like blue but softer and wet is the colour we know
    to be grey,

That feels much like rain, hung low in a cloud with tones of soft
    gentle clay.

It's a fog that is filled with our history, it's a spirit that speaks
    of our past.

It's a feeling of something quite eerie and yet—it's a feeling we all
    want to last.

*I remember the first time that I saw this grey—this mist hanging
    over the sea.*

*I remember wondering if any were lost: as I looked, were they
    searching for me?*

*I remember my thoughts and my words that cold day weren't as
    clear to me as was the sound,*

*Of the moaning and calling of distant fog horns, like a crying with
    no one around.*

A Place to Ponder

To say that our vision of white is in snow won't come as a
  total surprise.

As so many people in Canada say, our white is snow that dazzles
  the eyes.

But the feature that makes our white so unique is its placement far up
  in the sky.

Where it crowns all the mountains through most of B.C.
  to be seen as they tower up high.

*I remember discovering the beautiful Kootenays that seemed to be
  lost in the clouds.*

*I remember my smile when I found the Cascades as they stood out
  serene and so proud.*

*I remember my seeking the Lions out, and the thrill as I found them
  that night.*

*I now know for sure that the beauty of mountains is found in the
  colour of white.*

Winter's Bluff

To learn of our brown, you will have to go into the heart of our
   wonderful land,

And gaze at the hills just north of Penticton and its beaches of hot
   summer sand.

What highlights this brown is the contrast in colours of the hills and
   the endless blue lake,

And the green of the orchards that run alongside them, that's the
   depth that our colour brown takes.

Cloudscape

To seek out our purple you'll have to go down to the beach anytime
of the year,

To discover the starfish washed up by the sea or clinging tight
to the pier.

Morning Berth

Further Down the Road

You can wait for the spring when our cherry trees bloom and the pink
petals snow down on you.

Fall Upon the Land

If you're here in the fall you'll find orange in the leaves of our
maples, but let me tell you…

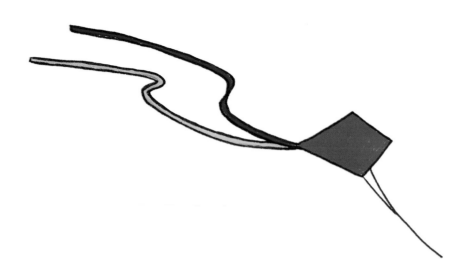

The truth of our colour is *not* just in flowers, in lakes or in valleys,
    in winter or summer.

It's *not* just in mountains nor in our tall green trees.

It's *not* in red sunsets or small busy quaint quays.

It's *not* just our wondrous gardens.

It's *not* just our mountain trails.

It's more than our B.C. fruit.

It's more than our salmon or whales.

The truth of our colour is found on the faces of all of the people
    you'll meet,

Out on the slopes or deep in the valleys or moving about
    on the street.

And though we look different, we all share the same dream, the
    forests, the mountains, the sea.

Boasting the wondrous beauty of nature through all of the colours
    of B.C.

Sea Wall See People

Lights of Old